To Chris Kubie, crane music interpreter
—J.C.G.

For Willie
—W.G.M.

Jean Craighead George would like to thank:
Dr. Paul A. Johnsgard, crane expert
Charlie Craighead, crane finder

Wendell Minor would like to thank:
Nature photographer Tom Mangelsen for the use of several of his crane photographs as visual reference
for the paintings in this book, Jean Craighead George and her family for sharing the wonderful
experience of viewing five hundred thousand cranes on the Platte River, and Remy Konitzer, helicopter pilot
extraordinaire, for giving the artist a crane's eye view of the Earth.

For further information about sandhill cranes you may visit these websites:
International Crane Foundation: www.savingcranes.org
Muleshoe National Wildlife Refuge: www.fws.gov/southwest/refuges/texas/muleshoe/index.html
Rowe Sanctuary, Platte River, Nebraska: rowesanctuary.org

"No! No! No!" the girl shouted, and waded into the water. She frightened Luck. He flapped to a grassy slope and landed, pointing his beak skyward.

KHARRRR. Wise dropped down beside him. They lifted their wings and leaped high in the air.

The girl picked up the plastic six-pack holder and smiled as the cranes danced.

"Luck," she called to the graceful bird, "I've just changed your name to Love."

KHARRRR.

KHARRRR.

The cranes told her their real names and went on dancing.

Above Route 70 a flock of motorcycles appeared. He remembered and followed them to Route 183 and on to Route 283.

There stood the windmill. Now he truly knew where he was, and he flew straight to the Texas marsh and looked for his "home," the girl with the blue glasses who had saved his life. She was not there. He kept flying.

A plastic six-pack holder glistened in the reeds below. Luck flew to it. The bird-watcher was on the boardwalk. Beside him stood the girl. She was not wearing her blue sunglasses.

Over Kansas Luck turned east to find the boy and the
canoe. Wise did not follow. She came down to rest in the
reeds in the Cheyenne Bottoms.

KHARRRR, Luck called for her. No answer. He was lost
again. He flew west looking for a baby carriage. But no baby
carriage was to be found.

In late August Luck and Wise flew back across the Bering Strait. Luck heard no foghorns. He was lost. Wise was not. She recalled the angle of the sun's rays and bugled, *KHARRRR*. Luck followed the love song.

When they came to the snow-covered Alaskan peaks, Luck brought them down into the tundra wetlands to sleep. By day he led them across Canada and then the Dakotas.

Then Luck saw the Platte River, but its magic was sleeping until spring. Luck and Wise kept flying south.

The three cranes flew into a dense fog over the Bering Strait. They followed the angle of the sun's rays, as their ancestors had done. Luck memorized the sound of foghorns on ships.

In Siberia Luck was back where he had been born!

His parents started a new family. Luck flew west. He winged over a marsh. Below, a female crane was calling for a mate. Luck parachuted to her side. He bowed. She bowed back. It was June. By the end of the summer they were a pair. Her name was Wise. Luck and Wise danced and composed their own song.

KHARRRR.

KHARRRR. This song would keep them together for as long as they lived.

The children went back to their games.

By the time the farmers were tilling the soil, Luck and all the sandhill cranes were far north. A few went to Wyoming and on west. Others winged north into Canada—some went to Manitoba and Saskatchewan. Some flew on to Hudson Bay. Luck and his parents went straight up the Rocky Mountain chain to Alaska. There were no roads with malls and baby carriages, so Luck memorized the snowcapped mountains of the Brooks Range.

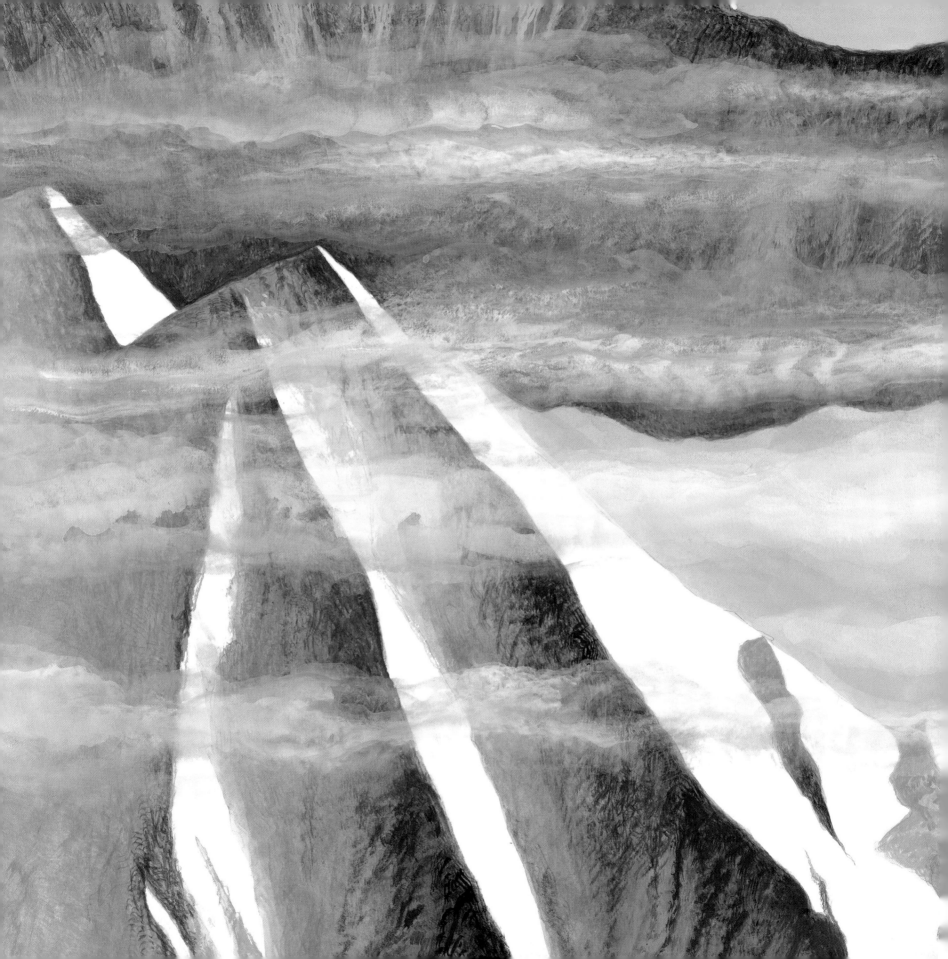

At dusk Luck and the thousands of cranes flew back to the spot where he had slept. Luck's space was taken by two *HKKKKKKKKK*ers. Their wings hit him. Their beaks struck at him. He jumped up, spread his wings, and hung above the cranes like a kite. Then a gentle wind carried him upriver.

CRACKAARR. Luck's voice was changing. It was deep. Would his parents recognize his new voice?

CRACKAARR. They knew him! Luck parachuted down. His parents jumped in the air. Throwing back their heads, they all danced for joy.

For almost two weeks Luck and his parents and five hundred thousand other cranes flew from the river to the fields, and from the fields to the river. Then they were gone.

*C*rackaarr, Luck called.

HKKKKKKKKKK, trumpeted the cranes around him. He heard no *CRACKAARR*s from his parents.

Crackaarr, he called again.

HKKKKKKKKKK.

Luck was lost. He waded slowly and deliberately into the shallow river, then stood still. Thousands of cranes gathered around him, trumpeting and flapping. The sun set. Night came. Luck called for his parents once more. No answer. Tired from his long flight, he tucked his beak into his back feathers, stood on one leg, and slept.

The sun came up. The cranes flew and came down in a cornfield.

Luck was hungry. He fed on fallen kernels of corn and soybeans from last autumn's harvest. He chased bugs and ate them.

Luck soared, dipped, and glided. He made designs in the sky with the other cranes. Somehow he remembered the river, although he had never been there before. It was an old memory—about twenty million years old.

Luck let down his long legs, cupped his wings, bowed his tail, and gracefully parachuted into the waters of the Platte River.

The old cranes steered the young back to Route 183 in northern Kansas and then on to Nebraska. In the distance, like a star on the horizon, the Platte River shone silver-gold. When Luck saw the magic river, he called out, *Crackaarr!*

And five hundred thousand cranes joined in, their voices like wind trumpets, swelling to a choir and then to a symphony.

The children in the school yards in Kearney, Nebraska, heard the symphony and stopped playing games. "Here come the cranes!" they shouted. "Spring is here!"

Farmers heard the ancient voices and readied their tractors for plowing. Bird-watchers saw them and cheered. Photographers snapped pictures.

Luck looked down on Route 70 in Kansas and memorized a pack of motor-cycles. Suddenly a storm struck, and the cranes were blown far off course. When the storm was over, Luck memorized a boy in a canoe on the Little Blue River.

Ten thousand more cranes joined Luck and his parents above the wetlands of Cheyenne Bottoms in Kansas. They came from Mexico, Louisiana, Nevada, and Arizona. Some had flown in from Florida. There were young cranes like Luck, with no red caps, and old cranes, all headed north. They formed a ten-mile line, three miles wide.

Luck and his parents soared across the Texas border, memorizing the hills and rivers below. Above Cherokee, Oklahoma, hundreds of cranes from Mexico joined them.

Luck circled a windmill.

By the time he had it memorized, his parents were far ahead.

Crackaarr, crackaarr, Luck trilled over and over.

CRACKAARR, CRACKAARR. His parents' voices! Their red crowns caught his eye. Luck caught up with them over a shopping mall in Kansas. His parents memorized the cornfields around the mall. Luck memorized a baby carriage.

It was March. Luck's parents were preparing for their long migration north to their nesting grounds. They were memorizing the reeds and waters of their winter home for their return in autumn. But Luck was memorizing the blue sunglasses on the face of the girl who had saved his life. To Luck she had become home.

O nce freed, Luck trilled to his parents.

Crackaarr!

CRACKAARR! his parents trumpeted from the sky.

The young crane spiraled up to meet them.

Together they circled the Texas marsh.

A young sandhill crane spread his six-foot wings and flew away.

"Good-bye, Luck!" called the girl who had set him free.

"That's not his name," said a bird-watcher. "In Asia, where I come from, a crane is called Love."

"Love is a beautiful name," said the girl, "but any bird that sticks its head in a plastic six-pack holder is going to need more luck than love."

Luck

Jean Craighead George   PAINTINGS BY Wendell Minor

LAURA GERINGER BOOKS
An Imprint of HarperCollins*Publishers*

Luck

Text copyright © 2006 by Julie Productions Inc.

Illustrations copyright © 2006 by Wendell Minor

Manufactured in China.

Library of Congress Cataloging-in-Publication Data

George, Jean Craighead, date

Luck / by Jean Craighead George ; paintings by Wendell Minor. — 1st ed.

p.   cm.

Summary: A young sandhill crane, Luck, finds his place in the ancient crane migration from northern Canada to the Platte
River.

ISBN-10: 0-06-008201-1 — ISBN-10: 0-06-008202-X (lib. bdg.)

ISBN-13: 978-0-06-008201-7 — ISBN-13: 978-0-06-008202-4 (lib. bdg.)

1. Sandhill crane—Juvenile fiction.   [1. Sandhill crane—Fiction.   2. Cranes (Birds)—Fiction.]   I. Minor, Wendell, ill.
II. Title.

PZ10.3.G316Luc 2006

[Fic]—dc22   2004015628
                                                                                                                            CIP
                                                                                                                            AC

Typography by Alicia Mikles

1 2 3 4 5 6 7 8 9 10

❖

First Edition

Hudson
Bay

*Atlantic
Ocean*

Platte River,
Nebraska

UNITED STATES
OF AMERICA

Texas Marshland

*Gulf of
Mexico*

MEXICO